Farmers
Market
→

We know how.

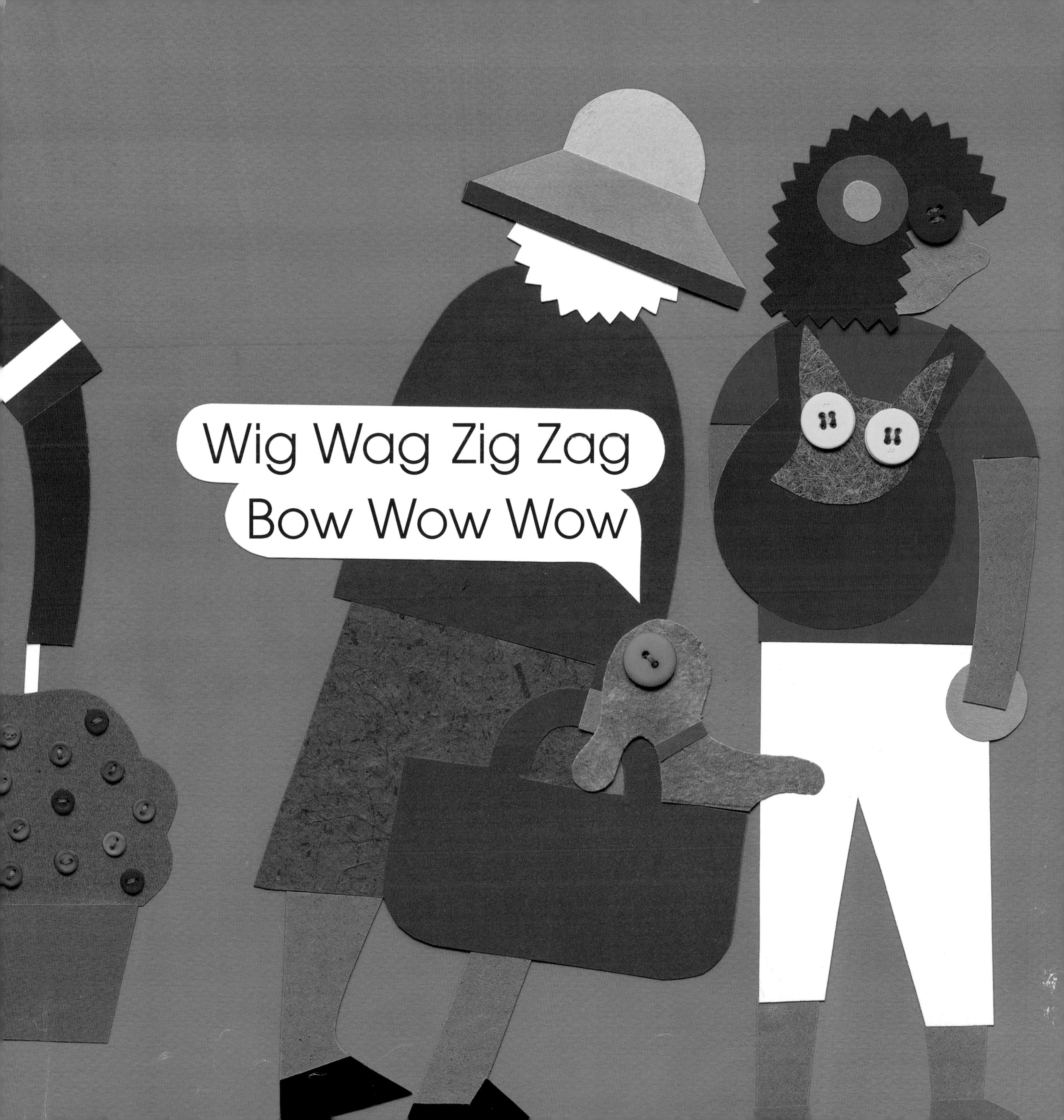
Wig Wag Zig Zag
Bow Wow Wow

Wag
a tail.
Wag
a tail.

We
know
how.

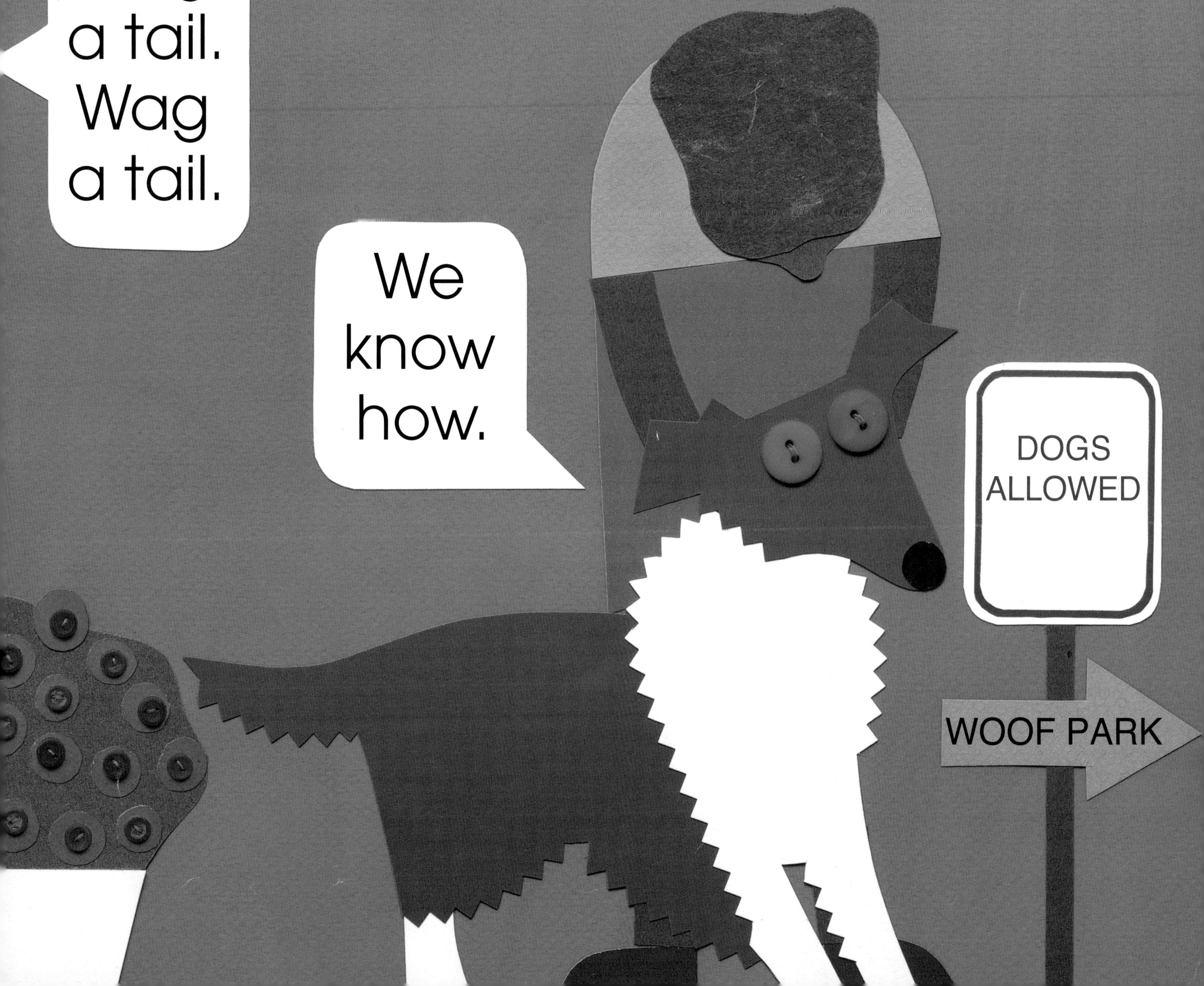

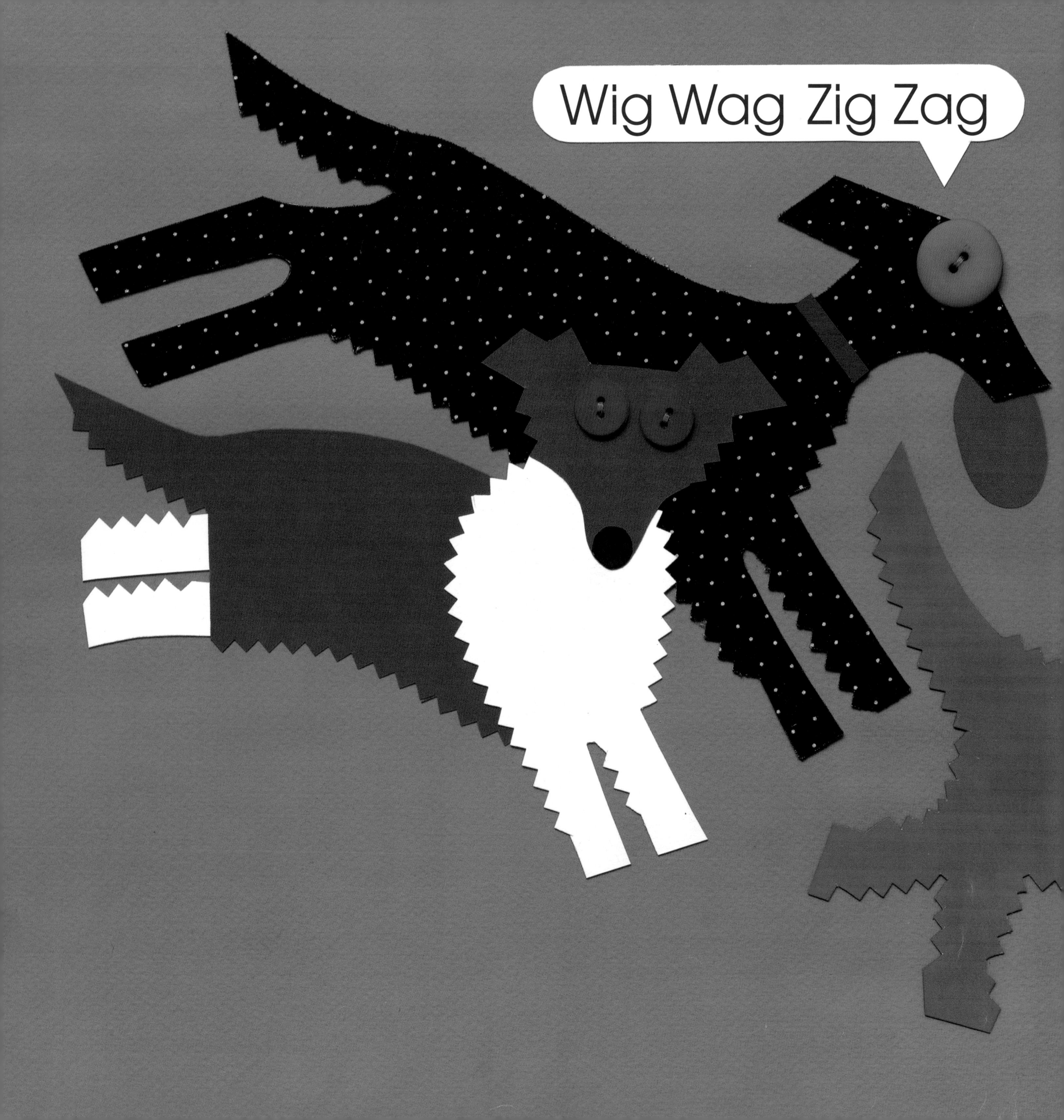
Wig Wag Zig Zag

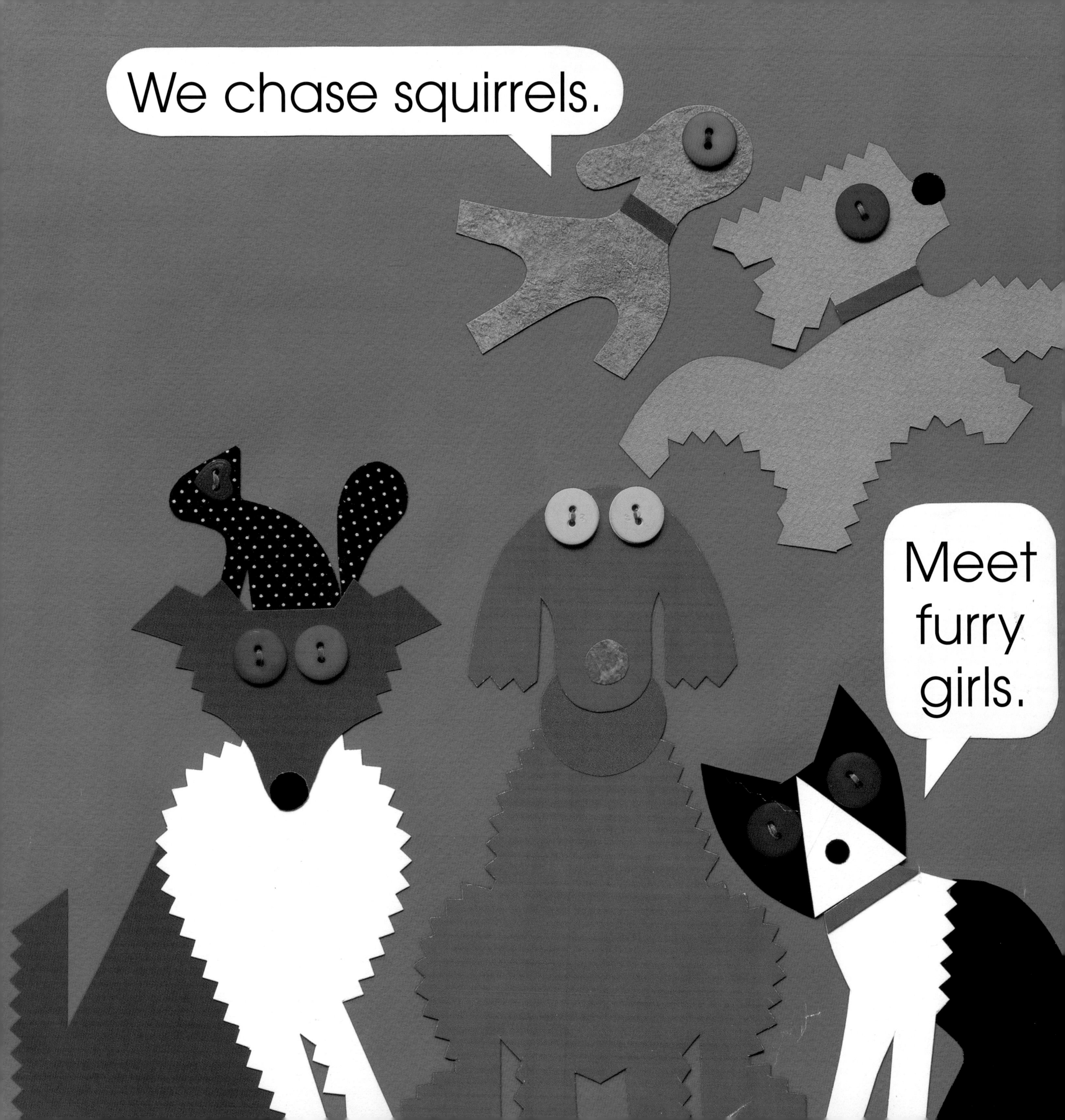
We chase squirrels.
Meet furry girls.

But we *never* drool.

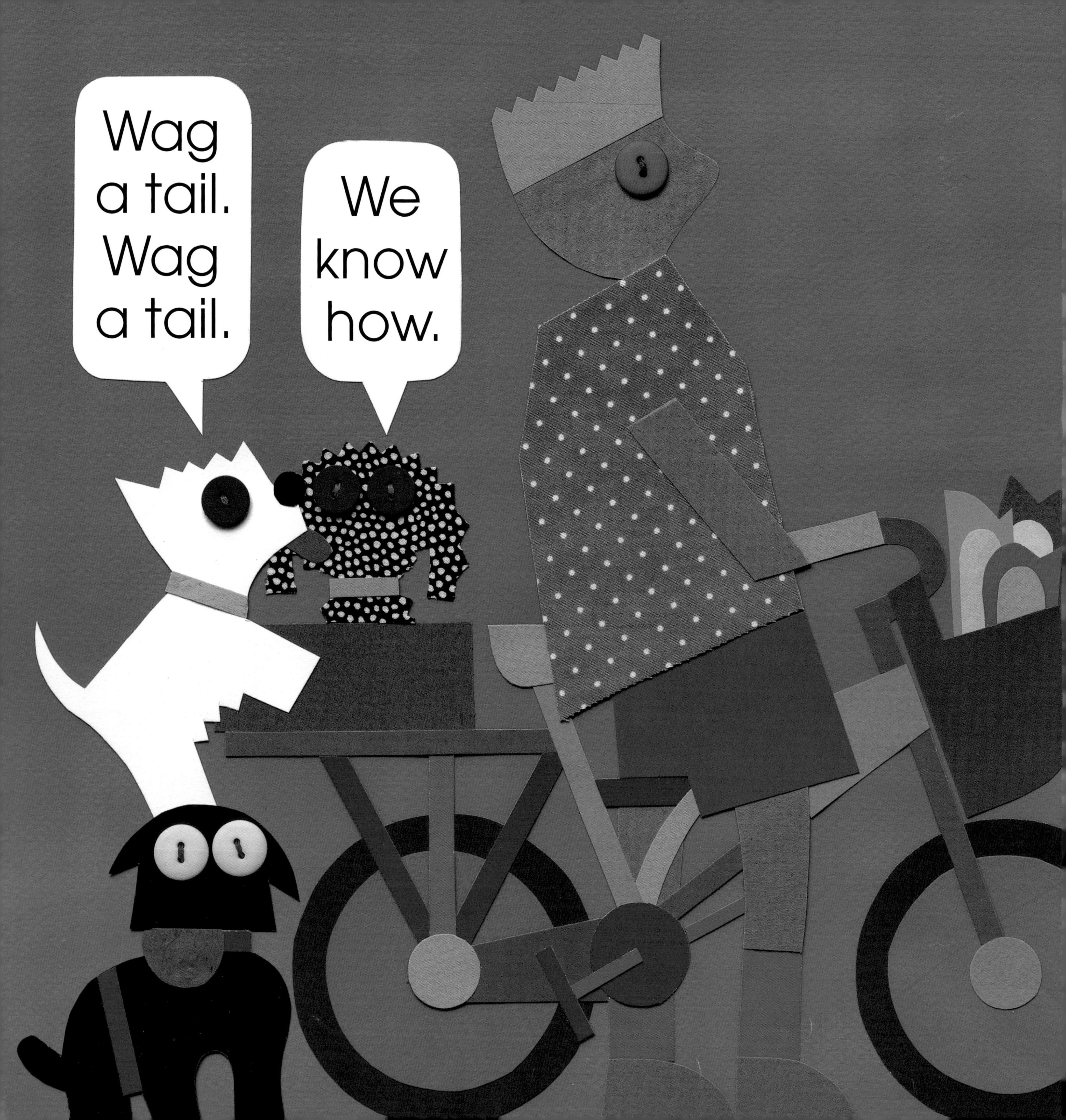
Wag a tail. Wag a tail.
We know how.

Bow Wow School Graduates

NAME: Spike
FAMILY: Unknown
Lively, fun loving, high energy. May chase small animals, likes to howl. Keep an eye on Spike, he needs more obedience training.

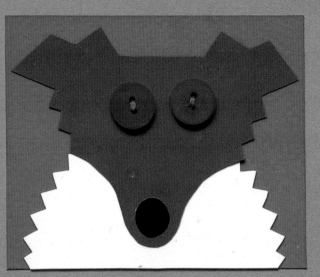

NAME: Queenie
FAMILY: Collie
Smart. Loves children, friendly, wants to please. Doesn't need much exercise, but needs brushing.

NAME: Oscar
FAMILY: Dachshund
Loves to be involved in family activities. Clever, but easily bored. Likes city living, enjoys long walks in the park.

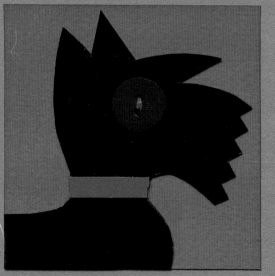

NAME: Lucky
FAMILY: Scottish Terrier (Scottie)
Independent, spunky. Barks a lot, would be a good watchdog. Needs exercise, may chase small animals.

NAME: Fluffy
FAMILY: Irish Setter
Needs exercise, happy when she can run and play.

NAME: Rufus
FAMILY: Labrador Retriever
Kind, outgoing, likes to please. Loves to retrieve balls and Frisbees.